AN AFRICAN NIGHT'S ENTERTAINMENT

Cyprian Ekwensi

AFRICAN READERS' LIBRARY

John Murray

Text copyright © Cyprian Ekwensi 1962, 1996
Illustrations copyright © Pilgrim Books Ltd 1971, 1996

This edition first published 1996 under licence from African Universities Press
by John Murray (Publishers) Ltd
50 Albemarle Street, London W1X 4BD

Text and cover design by Neville Poulter Design
Cover illustration by Anneke Lipsanen
Typesetting by Neville Poulter
Reproduction by Cape Imaging Bureau cc
Printing and binding by CTP Book Printers, Parow

ISBN 0-7195-7126-X

CONTENTS

4

'Put your money on this sheepskin,' said the old man, 'and if, by the time I finish my tale, there is one of you awake, that man shall claim everything we have collected.'

Young men, old men, children, women: they all put some money on the sheepskin beside the old story teller. He waited till they had sat down. He himself settled comfortably on the *catifa* and smiled.

'It is a long tale of vengeance, adventure and love. We shall sit here until the moon pales and still it will not have been told. It is enough entertainment for a whole night:

AN AFRICAN NIGHT'S ENTERTAINMENT.'

CHAPTER ONE

THE DREAM

There was once a man called Mallam Shehu. He was a rich man, richer than anybody else who lived at the time. Wealth was the gift that Allah had given him; and he had three wives, but of children he had none and was unhappy for that reason. Whenever he said his prayers, he did not ask Allah to give him a son or daughter of any particular talent, but any child, someone he could look upon as his own.

One night when he was asleep he dreamed that he went to market. There he saw a man selling a horse. Now Shehu liked the horse and when he heard that someone had already bought it for three pounds, he offered the seller three pounds ten shillings. The man who had already bought the horse was offended and he said:

'Mallam, why do you want to deprive me of my bargain?'

'Not so, my friend. I want the horse. You want the horse. The seller wants money. To whom should he sell?' Mallam Shehu paid

for the horse and on his way home he felt very happy.

When he got home he showed the horse proudly to his servants and to all who knew him.

At night he dreamed that the horse had a foal. The foal grew up and Shehu loved it as he had loved its mother. As soon as it was rideable he ordered his servants to saddle it so that he might have the honour of mounting it first.

The servants saddled and bedecked the young horse as best they could, and Shehu mounted. He rode out into the fields where he spurred her into a gallop. The horse stumbled; Shehu fell, breaking an arm and a leg. Then he woke from his dream.

He was wet with sweat. He could not sleep any longer. He got up and began to walk about the room, thinking. His breathing became loud and laboured. An attendant came into his bedroom and asked him what was wrong. Why had he got up in the middle of the night, holding his head in his hands and thinking so deeply? 'Go away!' he said. 'Nothing is wrong with me. In the morning you will call Mallam Sambo to me.'

Mallam Sambo was the man with the greatest knowledge of herbs at the time. He was also said to be able to interpret dreams. Mallam Shehu believed in him implicitly.

'Yes,' said Sambo, when he had heard Shehu's story. 'Allah has shown you what he has in store for you, as you can see from the dream. That foal you saw in the dream stands for your future wife. Just as you got to the market when someone had already bought the horse, so also will you be late in courting your future wife. You'll find that somebody has already betrothed her; but if you're lucky, you may still win her from the man. She is the only girl who is likely to give you a child. But when she has borne you a baby you will suffer so much that you will regret having gone against the will of Allah. In my opinion, it is best to let the matter rest as it is. Do not concern yourself with marriage. For you it was not written that way.'

'Will Allah indeed let me see a son of my own?' Mallam Shehu exclaimed. 'If so, I do not care how much I suffer after that!'

'Remember this, Mallam Shehu: Allah is there to grant us our requests.'

'You speak truth, Mallam Sambo. But how am I to know the girl?'

'You will have to search for her. When you see her, you will know.'

'Thank you,' said the rich man. 'Please take this money for explaining my dream to me.'

'No, Mallam. My father taught me never to accept money for practising my art. I go now.'

Mallam Sambo bowed and left the room.

The servants made enquiries. They found that Mallam Audu was indeed the father, and that the girl's name was Zainobe. They came back and told Mallam Shehu. Shehu sent a message to the girl, asking her to come and see him. The servants went to the girl and gave her the message. She said: 'Who is this Mallam Shehu, and what does he want with me?'

'We do not know,' said the servants. 'He only sent us to fetch you.'

'Go and tell him I shall not come.'

Now this girl Zainobe had been betrothed to Mallam Abu Bakir ever since she was a mere infant. The man had put some money in a pot and poured water into it as a sign that both of them would grow up together as husband and wife. Both of them had loved each other deeply. She grew up to be very beautiful; so beautiful that her mother began to doubt whether Abu Bakir was worthy of her.

The time approached when she would have to go to the home of Abu Bakir, but his people were not yet quite ready to receive her. It was during this time that Mallam Shehu's servant saw her.

Mallam Shehu kept sending messages to the girl to come and see him, and at last Zainobe asked him to state what he wanted of her.

'Tell him that I am not a man. I cannot come alone to see him. That is not proper.'

Shehu sent back word that he wanted to marry her. She told him that she was already betrothed and that nothing would ever separate her from her fiancé, except Allah.

'I have grown up to think of Abu Bakir as my husband; my parents and the parents of Abu Bakir arranged it all when I was a child playing in the sand,' was the message she sent him.

The news of Mallam Shehu's demand soon got to Abu Bakir. He could not eat; he could do nothing throughout that day until he had spoken to her.

'Zainobe, I have heard that the richest man in this town wants to marry you.'

'And what did your informer tell you my reply was to him?'

'If I heard aright, they said you told him that you would marry no one else but me; but Zainobe, I am afraid of women. Women are like water, and horses.'

13

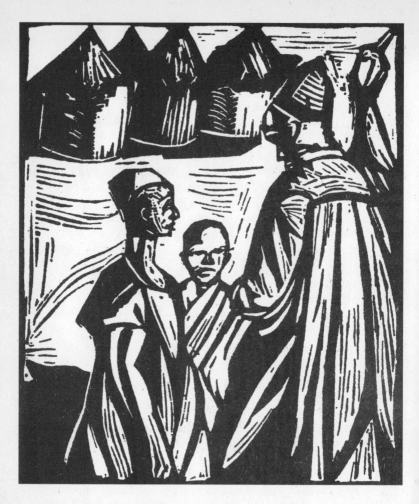

'I don't understand your proverb.'

'Women are like water, because you cross a stream in the dry season and when you return in the rains the same stream will drown you. If you love a horse very much and you feed her, when you come to ride her, she'll throw you down and break your backbone. So is a woman's love. Dry today like the ebb tide; high tomorrow like a flood.'

Zainobe said: 'You speak of deep things, Abu. But I'm not that kind of woman. Nothing will ever make me marry Mallam Shehu, unless he's prepared to marry my dead body.'

Abu's heart gladdened at this, and they began to play just as if

14

they were still children. They were playing when one of Mallam Shehu's servants came to Zainobe. Abu answered him, 'Come in, and let me hear your message. What do you want?'

The servant said: 'I am sent to Zainobe, not to you.'

Abu took a stick and beat the boy. He ran back to his master and reported, 'I met Abu Bakir there and was very lucky to escape with my life.'

'Is that so?' Shehu was angry. He who was so rich that everybody feared him – who was Abu Bakir to treat him in this manner? Shehu determined to show Abu Bakir that he was a rich man. He sent for Mallam Sambo, and Mallam Sambo came.

'That dream you interpreted to me is coming true at last. I have seen the girl, and everything is going according to your prediction.'

'All right: if you follow my advice, you'll leave the girl alone, and stay as Allah created you.'

'No,' said Mallam Shehu. 'I can't do that. I'll go mad. Even in my dreams I see this girl, though I've not seen her in the flesh.'

'What then do you want?'

'I want to marry her.'

'Listen, this is what you must do. Get me the musk from a deer and then I'll see that everything is all right.'

'Nothing else?'

'Nothing else. When I go home, send your boys, and I'll give a secret and alluring preparation to them. Then find some way to have Zainobe's body smeared with it. As soon as that is done the girl is bound to fall in love with you.'

The Mallam found no difficulty in getting the musk from a deer. He gave it with his instructions to a trusted servant who took it to the girl and came back to report that he had persuaded her to smear her body with the scent, which had delighted her.

CHAPTER THREE

ZAINOBE IS LOVESICK

Zainobe, all fragrant with the perfume, went to her mother as soon as the servant had left. 'Abu Bakir has sent for me,' she lied. 'I must go at once.'

'You know your father does not want you to leave the house in the afternoon. But luckily he is away: please do not do anything that will hurt the reputation of your family.'

Zainobe ran into the house at once and washed her feet and hands. She dressed herself in her best clothes and ran all the way to the house of Mallam Shehu. There were many people in the rich man's house, and, when he saw her from a distance, he ordered one of the servants to conduct her to the seventh room in his household. He was so pleased to see her that he left the great men who had come to see him and went into the seventh room.

One of these men got up at once and ran to Abu Bakir.

17

'We saw your betrothed in the house of the wealthy Mallam Shehu. We do not know why she has gone there ...'

Meanwhile Mallam Shehu greeted the girl and told her that she had been wounding him.

'I have no time for long words,' said the girl. 'I left home under a pretext; my father has forbidden me to come out in the afternoon. He will be very angry if he finds out that I left home. Say what you have to say, and let me go.'

'Why do you speak to me like that? Do you not like me?'

'If I disliked you, would I leave my home to come alone to your house? Tell me what you have to say; the time is short.'

Mallam Shehu said: 'I want you to be my wife.'

Zainobe laughed: 'The question of marriage cannot arise between us.'

'Remember, Zainobe, that Abu is a poor man. If you marry me, you will be free from want. Your parents will have everything that money can buy.'

'My parents have never depended on you for money. So, don't

18

talk like that, I beg of you. All blessings come from above. You have been blessed with money, but there are people who do not know of it nor do they even care: your riches mean nothing to their lives.'

Mallam Shehu was baffled. The girl held him and his riches in contempt. For a moment he gazed at her. Then he remembered the scent Mallam Sambo had prepared for him.

'Take this,' he said, offering some more of it to her. 'Surely you cannot refuse this? It is not money, but a scent of no consequence. It is a shame that you should visit a person like Mallam Shehu and go away empty-handed.'

The charm of the scent changed Zainobe's mood. She took it from him and went home. Fortunately her father had not returned, but she learnt that Abu had called in her absence and, having waited for her, had left without seeing her.

♒

CHAPTER FOUR

A CLOTH IN THE MARKET-PLACE

Zainobe's mother asked her where she had been and she said she had been to the house of Abu Bakir.

'That is a lie! Abu has been here all the time, waiting for you to return.'

Zainobe stamped her foot angrily. 'So it has come to that? He follows me around to know where I have been. Is that it? I know that Abu has been wanting an excuse to quarrel with me for a long time now. You say I have not been to see him; was it not he who gave me this scent?'

'Let me see,' said the mother.

She took the scent and smeared some of it on her face, then smiled affectionately. When she spoke again Zainobe was surprised to note her change of attitude.

'I've been wanting to tell you something,' she confided. 'Some

time ago the Shehu sent for you, but I did not tell you what he wanted with you because your father was so angry with him. Actually, the Mallam wants to marry you, and I don't see any reason why he shouldn't. Of course, people will think it is his money that is attracting you, and that is why I have been hesitating. Look at Abu Bakir; he has spent his time with us ever since he was a child, but how much money has he ever brought into the family? Such things are important, you know.'

Zainobe said: 'I rather like this Mallam Shehu; he is a man who knows how to get what he wants. Dear mother, I am afraid to admit this before my father because I know he might kill me. But if Mallam Shehu marries me, none of you will ever want for anything in this world again; you won't have to smoke yourself in the kitchen or wear rags.'

'How shall we do it, then?'

'The next time Mallam Shehu sends somebody to speak to me, we must encourage the man with some good news.'

Meanwhile Mallam Shehu sent for his adviser, Mallam Sambo, and told him that he had succeeded in giving the scent to the girl.

'Watch and see what happens next,' Sambo said. 'It is like setting fire to gunpowder. There'll be an explosion soon.'

Shehu continued to send messages to the girl to come and see him, and his messengers were not driven away. At last Zainobe replied that she was willing to marry him. The servant went home delighted, and delivered the message to the Shehu. He was extremely happy.

Abu Bakir returned to the house of Zainobe, and found her in. He sent greetings to the girl, and asked her to come to the room where they used to sit together. For a long time she did not appear, and when at last she came her face was long and sad. Abu, too, was not in a good frame of mind.

They sat for a long time, then Abu asked: 'Why don't you greet me?'

'Because you don't seem pleased with me. It is written in your face. If you have anything to tell me, do so; I am doing some work in the house with my mother.'

'You've never spoken to me before in this manner, Zainobe.'

'Have you ever come here at such an awkward time?'

'There is no clock for me in this house. It has always been open to me at all hours of the day.'

'I know that, but I'm working now. Tell me what you want to say. I am very busy now, and if you have nothing to say, let me go.'

Abu Bakir was silent, trying to control his rising temper.

'I heard that you went to visit the richest man in this district; I knew it as soon as you entered his *Zaure*. Nothing is hidden under the sun. I ran here at once and asked your mother where you'd gone, and she told me you'd been to see me. I couldn't wait here and catch you returning because I was so angry. If I had been able to control myself, I might have waited here and seen you return. Then I should have flogged you thoroughly.'

'Has it come to flogging?'

'Yes. I have heard such talk before about your movements, and when I asked you, you denied it. I gave you a proverb which you said you did not understand. Remember?'

'I remember the proverb and the answer I gave you when you had explained it to me. Now you listen to me. When a trader has got hold of some good cloth and has taken it to the market, at least ten bidders will price it before he sells it to the highest bidder. You must understand that a girl who has not been married is like a cloth in the market-place. You are only the first person to demand my hand in marriage. Do you imagine that means that you are definitely going to be my husband?'

Abu grew hot with anger, but he was afraid to annoy the father of the girl by flogging her. Leaving her abruptly, he went to her father and laid his complaint before him.

'Don't worry,' said the old man. 'My wife and I will never change towards you. Death is the only agent that will prevent your marrying Zainobe. Do not have foolish fears like a little boy! Is Zainobe not my daughter? Must she not do my will?'

'I agree with you in many ways, father; and your words bring me hope. But I must tell you that Zainobe is not going to marry me. I have read it from her ways.'

'Don't say that again.'

'Since I have been coming here, I have always regarded you as a father. Have I ever before spoken in this manner to you? But listen – Zainobe has just told.me her mind; and I understand proverbs.'

'What proverb have you in mind?'

'Well, Zainobe told me that she is like a cloth in the market, that it is not everybody who offers a price for her that will get her.'

24

The old man's eyes kindled with anger. He sprang up to call the girl's mother, and at that moment he heard a quick movement behind the door.

'Who is hiding behind that door? Who has been listening to our talk?'

He went behind the door and looked but saw nobody and a moment later the girl joined him.

'Zainobe, what did you say to Abu?'

'I told him that a woman without a husband is like a cloth in the market; that the first man to woo her may not be the one who will marry her.'

'Are you in your senses?'

'Why shouldn't I be in my senses?'

The old man seized a cane and began to thrash her. She cried aloud, and her mother came in.

'Why do you flog my daughter? Is it because of Abu Bakir? You cannot force the girl to marry a man because you like him; give her a chance to choose the man she likes.'

'What!' gasped the old man. 'You! To speak thus to me? Haven't we been agreed all these years? Has something happened to you?'

He pushed her away from him so that he might swing his cane at her and Zainobe at the same time. Abu intervened.

'Don't flog them. Women behave like donkeys; a donkey will know that it is doing the wrong thing, but by flogging it you will not prevent it from repeating the same thing tomorrow. Zainobe's father heard these words and stopped.

When Abu got home he told his parents what had happened.

'Didn't we warn you all the time that this girl would never marry you?' his mother said. 'I didn't try to argue with you because your eyes were veiled with the film of love. Abu, my son, go and sit down and don't worry yourself any longer. If it is the will of Allah that you should marry her, you will; if not, whatever you do, love alone will never help you.'

Abu was obstinate. 'I am not going to listen to this, mother. I shall not live in this town and see Zainobe in another man's house. I'm telling you this so that whatever I do in the future will not surprise you.'

CHAPTER FIVE

A MARRIAGE AND A BIRTH

Mallam Shehu was in his house when the message came to him that he should produce the bride-price for his marriage to Zainobe. Zainobe and her mother were willing to accept his proposal.

Shehu produced the bride-price, but the father of the girl was bent on her not marrying him. 'I shall not live to see any other man than Abu marry Zainobe,' he declared.

The people returned with the gifts they had taken to the girl's father and the advisers of Mallam Shehu told him not to be discouraged: 'Since the girl and her mother are quite willing, there's nothing to fear.'

Mallam Shehu distributed money among the relatives of the girl, and sent a good portion to the king of the land. The king at once sent to Mallam Audu, the father of Zainobe, telling him not to be angry, that the girl could not be happy if she married a man she did not like.

'If you are using your power as king of this land to force me to accept your views in this matter,' said Mallam Audu, 'that is a different thing; but as long as I live, Abu is the man to marry Zainobe.'

The king made all arrangements for the marriage to take place, and sent the bride-price to Abu Bakir in payment of whatever money he might have deposited with the parents of the girl. Abu refused. 'I do not want one penny of her money.' That night, he spoke to his mother. 'This older brother of mine is quite able to take care of you. I am going away for a time, and if anything happens in my absence he'll do his best for you. Do not be afraid for me. I am going to have my vengeance, whatever happens; but it will have to be in my own particular way.'

'I don't like these words you're saying, my son.' She began to weep, and Abu tried to comfort her.

27

At dawn he called his brother and told him to take care of their mother. 'I am going away now. Don't ask me where I am going, because I do not know. I may be away for a week, I may be away for more; everything rests with Allah.'

He took his bows and arrows and nothing else, apart from a few pence which he had in his pocket. On bare feet he tramped away and was soon lost to sight.

Abu travelled for days and nights, working on the way, sleeping when he got to a village. Whenever he got to a new village his first enquiry was always whether there was anyone who knew how to wreak vengeance on men. And when they told him not to dare such things, that Allah alone could wreak vengeance, he left them, in anger, and went on.

In due time the wedding of Zainobe and Mallam Shehu took place. It was a lavish occasion: even the king had not spent so much money when he had married, nor had more distinguished guests ever attended a wedding. Zainobe remained in Shehu's house after the ceremony.

A year passed and then to Mallam Shehu's surprise and delight

Zainobe gave birth to a male child. There was great rejoicing, and Shehu at the naming ceremony called him 'Kyauta,' that is, 'Allah be Thanked'.

The boy grew fast. He was as handsome as his mother was beautiful. Mallam Shehu's outlook on life changed entirely. He who used to frown and brood now went about his work smiling, and radiating cheer and goodwill among men. He gave presents of money to all whom he met. In keeping with the custom, he sent away one of his wives, but he saw to it that she had enough to live on for the rest of her life, even if she did not marry again.

The circumcision came, and after that the child went to school. His manners were so good that people were attracted to him, and, despite the fact that his father was a rich man, they expressed their appreciation of his good breeding by giving him presents of money. He was not aloof to the poorer boys. He knelt down in greeting to all who were older than he, even to the brother of Abu Bakir, in front of whose house the road to the school lay.

His father built him a separate house within his own compound and there all his friends came to visit him and to play games with him.

CHAPTER SIX

THE QUEST FOR VENGEANCE

Mallam Abu Bakir was very tired. He lay in the shade of a tree, not knowing in which direction to bend his steps next.

Above him, hidden in the tree, a group of scowling men gazed down greedily, discussing what to do with him.

'Let us shoot him,' said one of these dark-visaged men.

'There's no need,' whispered the other. 'Let's take his property, but not his life. He looks quite harmless.'

The first man insisted, and, fixing an arrow to his bow, shot at the sleeping Abu, but missed. Abu started and sprang to his feet. He looked round and found no one. Then he looked up and saw the rogues leering at him.

'Are you a thief?' they asked.

'I am not,' answered Abu. 'I am a man who has been wronged. I am searching for someone to take revenge for me.' In a few words he told them his story of love and disappointment.

The thieves came down from the tree. The man who appeared to be their leader laughed heartily and, raising his hairy arm, struck Abu on the cheek. 'Coward!' he growled. 'Lazy fool! Is she the only woman in the world? Why can't you marry another?'

'Join us, and forget your sorrow,' one of them invited.

'I cannot steal,' Abu confessed.

He went on. Further down the road he heard drumming, *gwogie* music, and women singing. He asked a man what all the noise was about.

'You're nearing the town,' the man answered.

'Do you think I'll meet a mallam there who'll avenge my wrongs? It appears that the town is fairly big.'

'Ah!' exclaimed the man. 'You must be a stranger in these parts: that's why you ask such a question. Do you know the name of this town?'

'I don't.'

'The name is "Birnin Zauna da Shirin Ka"'. That is, "the land where everyone holds himself in a state of readiness". Day or night, afternoon or evening, the people of this town always know in advance when a strange thing is going to happen in the town. It is indeed a bad place.'

'So, if a man wants to do a bad thing to someone else, he'll find a man there to help him?'

'Of course! Thousands of them!'

'Very good. When I get there, whom should I ask for?'

'Ask for the king.'

When Abu got into the town, he asked the first man he met and that man said he was a stranger too. The next man told him that they had no king and that the man who ran the town was called: 'Tausayinka da Sauki', which means 'the sorrow in your heart is little'. Tausayi had gone there to seek refuge from his parents and from the people whom he had wronged, and since then the village had grown. Now it was peopled by men who had broken customary laws or were in some way afraid of punishment.

'Let us go to this Tausayinka da Sauki,' Abu suggested.

They went there. The man was out; he had been called away by an assassin. Tausayi's wife told Abu that this was a bad town where people did not do wrong in secret. Her own husband was a man whose services as a killer were highly sought. She led

32

Abu into a room and told him to wait.

'When he returns from his mission, he'll attend to you.'

Abu remained in the chair until tiredness overcame him, and he fell asleep. At about midnight Tausayi returned, and his wife told him he had a visitor.

'Bring him before me,' he ordered, and when Abu came he welcomed him and asked him his name and whether he had been well attended to by his wife.

'Where do you come from?' Tausayi then asked.

'A place called Galma.'

'Very well. Go and sleep, and tomorrow you can tell me what you want.'

Abu went to bed. That night the man consulted his oracle and before dawn he had discerned all that had happened to Abu Bakir and why he had come to this town of Zauna da Shirin Ka for help.

'What shall we do for him?' Tausayi asked his wife. 'Shall we let him go on suffering, or shall we help him?'

The woman said: 'If he agrees to your conditions, the best thing will be to help him.'

Next morning Abu met Tausayi.

'I did not sleep well last night,' Abu complained.

'Do not worry,' Tausayi advised him. 'I have been told all that I want to know about you. Do not be surprised. You are thinking of injuring Mallam Shehu for taking Zainobe from you. Your idea is that he has done so because he has more money than you. That idea is wrong. Mallam Shehu took the girl from you because he has looked for a son for thirty-five years in vain, and one night he dreamt that if he married your betrothed, she would bear him a son. And now the prophecy is fulfilled; Zainobe gave him a baby boy a few months ago. And believe me, Abu Bakir, if you were to set eyes on this child, you would never have the heart to harm one hair of his head. Go and rest, Abu. Zainobe still loves you, but she has a duty to her husband and her son which surpasses all love. Let Allah alone avenge you.'

Abu's blood ran cold. 'I thought I had reached the end of my journey,' he muttered to himself, 'and now, this man is telling me terrible things.' He looked up after a long time and said: 'Is there then no way by which I may get my revenge? I know that he married the girl because he wanted a child. But ...' and then an evil thought came to him, 'can't it be arranged that this same son should be the cause of his death?'

'That is not difficult. I could easily dispose of the man and his son, and make his money – that possession of his that has made him so conceited – I could make all his money run to waste; it is as easy as putting a light to dry thatch and watching it burn. But what I fear is the vengeance of Allah Himself.'

'I do not fear that,' Abu exclaimed. 'If that is the only difficulty, go ahead! Let me know that I've reached the end of my journey.'

Tausayi's head was bowed in thought. He lifted it slowly, fixing his gaze on the face of Abu Bakir. 'If I am to do anything, you must swear that when your wishes have been achieved the punishment shall be on your own head.'

'I agree!'

Tausayi brought out the Koran and put Abu Bakir through the ceremony of the oath. Then he said: 'There's only one thing I want.' He named a certain tree, and told Abu that he wanted the sap from this tree. In the forest where this species grew, no other tree ever stood near it because of its deadly nature.

'Where shall I find it?' Abu asked.

'You have to search for it. I know that it is somewhere near my own home. When I was a child my father used to tell me about it, but later I did evil and ran away from home to found this village for people of my kind. I shall help you though.' He thought hard for a little while, and said: 'When you leave here, make for a certain town called Kobonka Naka, that is, "your penny is yours". There you'll see my father, if he's still alive, and if you give him this he'll know that I sent you. Ask for my brother, and get him to help you find the tree.'

He gave Abu a charm, and, thanking him, Abu took it and departed.

34

CHAPTER SEVEN

TAUSAYI'S FATHER

Abu got to Kobonka Naka, and asked the people whether they knew the father of Tausayinka da Sauki. They looked at him as if he were mad. They asked him where he came from and he answered 'Birnin Zauna da Shirin Ka'.' He wandered around the town for over seven days until at last, exhausted, he fell down at the foot of a tree by the gate of the town. He took the charm out of the girdle round his waist and examined it. Certainly the charm had not been of very much use. He was still studying it when an old man came up, carrying a basket.

Abu saw how weak the man looked, and out of sheer pity offered him help. There was no knowing, either, whether he might not be able to get food from him to settle the growlings of his stomach. They soon fell into conversation and the old man asked

35

him where he came from. 'I am a little mad,' Abu confessed. 'I have come from Birnin Zauna da Shirin Ka', and was so foolish as not to ask my informer the name of his father, whom I must find.' He proceeded to relate what he remembered of his host's magic powers, noting out of the corner of his eye that the old man was not uninterested. Now and again he asked pertinent questions, saying that he had lost a son, and that for the last twenty-eight years he had not heard from the boy.

'No one has told me anything of his whereabouts.' He paused, and then said: 'This man you speak about, what does he look like?'

'He is tall and black, a big strong man, with a pointed nose and a big head ...' As he gave detail after detail the old man's eyes glowed brightly. 'What did you say was the name of this man?'

'Tausayinka da Sauki.'

'What is the town called?'

'Birnin Zauna da Shirin Ka'.'

'And you are a native of ...'

'Galma, my father.' The old man looked confused.

'I have never heard those names before. Your description of the man fits my son, but these names of yours ... I can't understand them. They are fictitious.'

'It is so, father. I have been foolish not to have tried to find out the real name of this man; but that is what they call him.'

While they were talking they made their way back to the old man's home, and, as Abu Bakir bent down to place the basket on the floor, the charm fell out of his pocket.

'Ah!' he exclaimed. 'I forgot. Here is a charm that the man gave me. He said that, if I showed it to his father, the old man would recognize it.'

A change came over the face of the old man as he took it and examined it. Tears stood in his eyes, and he muttered thickly: 'Allah's name be praised! I welcome you with my heart. He that has seen my son is indeed my son too.'

He gave Abu Bakir food and clothing, and that night they sat by the fire, talking.

'Where is the brother of your son?' Abu asked. 'I have a message for him.'

The brother soon appeared, and Abu told him that his brother wanted to see him. 'My mission here is to collect the sap of a certain tree that your brother has described to me. When I have done that, I shall return to Zauna da Shirin Ka'.'

'There need be no hurry about that,' said the old man. 'You can go soon enough. When you've rested, perhaps I can take you to the tree myself.'

Abu relaxed for two whole days. Then he became impatient, but now the old man did his best to persuade him not to go to the forest. 'No man I know,' he said, 'has ever gone there and come back alive. I have been in this Kobonka Naka for fifty years, and during that time many people have been to Kurmin Rukiki. Where are they? What happened to them?'

'I don't know, and I don't care either. If I must die, better to die in the quest than to live a coward.'

The old man thought to himself: 'If I let him go, I shall never get in touch with my son'.

'Listen, Abu,' he said. 'The best thing is this: take Tausayi's brother back to Zauna da Shirin Ka'. Then you can come back and continue your journey.'

'No, my father. I am going forward. I shall always go forward; never backward.'

The old man burst into tears. At that Abu took up the charm. and bade him goodbye. 'I have always been a wanderer. A wanderer I shall remain,' said Abu Bakir to himself.

Abu set out on his journey. He had not gone very far, when the old man called him back and apologized. 'Forgive me, Abu. But think of what it is not to see your son for nearly thirty years. Do not go away like this. Tomorrow will be a better day, for then you can have Tausayi's brother to guide you.'

Next day he gave Abu five pounds and a horse. 'These are for your food and your travel. This gourd you must use for storing the sap, for it must never be touched by the bare hands. My son will go with you part of the way on horseback. Goodbye.'

The son led him for a few miles till he came to the parting of the ways. 'Go ahead. You simply cannot miss your way. If you're in doubt, ask anyone you meet: "Where is Kurmin Rukiki?"'

Abu thanked him, and they parted.

38

CHAPTER EIGHT

THE ONE-EARED THIEF

Abu rode on, till the sweat was gumming his clothes to his body. In the full heat of the afternoon he stopped near a stream and ate some food. Then he led his horse down-stream, watered her, took off his clothes, and entered the water to bathe himself.

The water was cool and refreshing. He splashed it carelessly, and filled his treasured gourd with it. Presently he heard a hostile shout, 'Kai ... Kai!' and, when he turned round, two evil-looking men stood before him.

'What do you want?' he stammered.

'How did you get into this forest?' one of the men snarled. 'What are you doing?'

'I was hot and tired, and ... and I wanted to bathe ...'

'Come out of it, you fool!'

The man jumped in, and dragging Abu out, beat him severely. When he was almost senseless, both men left, taking with them his horse and his money. They walked away but suddenly turned and came back, as they said, '... to leave a mark on his body.'

'You seem very happy here,' said one of the men, when they got back. 'You're not even afraid of us. Don't you know that we are the most dreaded rogues of this area?'

Abu said: 'You have taken my money and my horse; what more do you want of me?'

'This!' said the man, and stepping forward, he cut off Abu's left ear. Then they left him.

Still Abu pressed forward. Late in the evening he met a number of men driving donkeys. He called out to them, and the men turned round and started to shout: 'Thief! Thief!'

'I am not a thief,' he pleaded. 'How can I be a thief?'

'Then who are you?'

Abu told them how the two men had robbed him of his money and cut off his left ear. He ended by begging them to take him into their company, since he was afraid to continue his journey alone. They agreed, and put him on a donkey. As a sign that he had been admitted into their brotherhood, they served him with food and water. 'People never travel alone in these parts,' they told him. 'They travel in tens and dozens.'

When they got to the market, Abu helped the merchants to sell their things. He sat in the stall until far into the night, when the gathering dispersed. The donkey-men thanked him for his services and left.

Abu was at a loss where to spend the night. He wandered from door to door, asking for shelter, but his cut ear was against him, and everybody who saw him thought he had lost it in a burglary. They called him a thief and shut their doors in his face. He had no alternative but to go to the market-place and sleep there.

At about midnight he heard shouts of 'Thief! Thief! ...' The alarm seemed to be coming from the centre of the town, but, as he got shakily to his feet, he realized that the voices were coming nearer and nearer. What was he to do?

He could not run away, for that would lead the men to suspect him; he did not dare rush towards them. Abu stood there, still half

41

asleep, half confused. Men rushed into the market-place. In a flash the thieves raced past him, and hot on their heels came the pursuers.

'This is the man! This is the man! ... Catch him!'

They seized the protesting Abu, and nothing he said or did could make them change their minds. Lights were shone on his face, and as soon as the men saw his ear they exclaimed: 'Look at his left ear! They cut it off when he went to steal.'

'Not so!' he argued. 'I ... I am no thief. I came here yesterday, and I had nowhere to stay.'

They led him to the house of the king and charged him with stealing. He denied ever having stolen anything in his life, and started to explain how a company of traders had brought him there. But no one would listen to him.

'Have you or have you not stolen the missing things?'

'I have not.'

'If you are an honest man, why did you not report yourself to the king as soon as you arrived? What stopped your mouth?'

Abu could answer nothing to this question, and they sentenced him to three months' imprisonment. The people whom Abu met in prison were very boastful. Every day, whenever they went to work under guard, they would recount how they had raided rich men, how they had swindled unsuspecting people, and what they hoped to do when they got back their freedom. Abu never said a word, nor joined in their conversation.

The warder was surprised at this. He asked Abu whether he had any feats of daring to recount, and Abu maintained time and time again that he was not a thief that he had been sentenced to jail for a crime he had not committed. The warder sympathized with him but could do nothing about it. He let Abu keep his gourd, useless though it seemed.

Abu served his three months without complaining. On the day of his release, he went to this sympathetic warder and made him an offer.

'I am in great difficulty,' he stated. 'I have not a penny in the world. Will you accept me as your servant, so that in a few months I can see what Allah has in store for me?'

The warder, in spite of friends warning him, received Abu with joy, and gave him a chance to reinstate himself. But the warder's friends kept on pestering him to remove Abu, asserting all the time that Abu was a thief, and that it was unthinkable that a warder should harbour a thief in his own household.

The warder's belief in Abu was not shaken. He tested Abu's honesty by giving him money to buy and sell things. Abu not only sold the goods, but brought back more profit than the warder had ever dreamt of. After a month, Abu, of his own initiative, added to his duties that of porter. Every penny he made he showed his master to avoid any form of suspicion. He kept this money on one side day after day until he was quite sure he had saved twenty shillings. That night he called his master aside and said:

'You have been very kind to me all this time. Do not think that I was ignorant of your friends' advice to you. I thank you for all your help. Here is my plan: when I was in jail, I told you how a certain Mallam Shehu had deprived me of my wife, and how I am on a mission of vengeance. The time has come for me to continue my journey.'

'My dear Abu,' said the warder, 'I thought you had forgotten all about that! You are quite happy here; why do you need to worry

yourself? You are not the only man who has ever been deprived of his betrothed. If you remain here with me, I can give you enough money and happiness to last you till the end of your life. Leave vengeance to Allah.'

'No,' said Abu. 'I cannot go back on my plans now: I have lost an ear; I have served three months' sentence; I have been robbed. It is too late to go back.'

The warder was deeply regretful. 'It has to be then?' he sighed. 'Prepare. I give you three days so that 1, too, may get certain things ready for you. How much money have you saved?'

'Twenty shillings, by my reckoning.'

'It is so.'

When three days had passed, the man brought out the twenty shillings that Abu had made as a porter and gave it to him. He added to this another sixty shillings, making a total of eighty shillings, gave him a horse and led him forth himself, some of the way.

'Ask for Kurmin Rukiki,' he said. 'You will never miss your way. I see you have not forgotten that gourd you seem to value so highly.'

They shook hands in the Muslim fashion, holding their hands for long intervals and smiting their breasts.

Allah bless you; my heart aches. I fear very much that you may never return.' Abu wheeled his horse and cantered away.

CHAPTER NINE

THE RETREATING FOREST

Abu went on till he came to the next village, and the first thing he did was to show himself to the king. The king received him as a very interesting and important person. He handed him over to a man who took great care of him. Abu remained in this town for three or four days. On the first night, thieves raided his host and Abu's horse and the money disappeared. He reported the matter to the king and the king gave orders that the thief should be sought; but the vigilance of the police went unrewarded, for in the end the culprits were not found, and Abu made up his mind not to wait there any longer.

His host advised him as many other hosts had done before him. 'Do not go to this Kurmin Rukiki. Those who go there never return. Leave vengeance for Allah to perform. Go back to your home.'

'Thank you; but I cannot go back. I would rather reach Kurmin Rukiki and die than take one step backwards.'

It was now some years since Abu had left home, and this was the fourth man to warn him. Still he remained firm. 'My resolve is to go forward all the time.'

The man gave him two pounds, saying that he was a mere messenger to the king. 'It is little, but I'm sure it will help you. It is wrong that you were deprived of your Allah-given wife.'

Before Abu left, the king of the town assisted him with one hundred shillings, a horse and clothes. He slept on the way and woke, and slept and woke, and still went on. He arrived at a certain village, the last outpost but one before the Kurmin Rukiki, a village remarkable for its poverty.

He got work as a goat-herd, earning milk and *fura* for his pains. The people regarded him with suspicion and many times he overheard them calling him a madman. 'If not, why does he say he's on his way to Kurmin Rukiki?'

One day he became tired of this life and he again asked them the way to Kurmin Rukiki. The people at last gave him a youth who took him to the top of a hill and pointed to a black patch, shimmering in the middle of rolling grassland. 'That is the Kurmior forest. Go to your death. I have never known a single man who went there and came back. They always pass through this village on their way. They never come back.'

He offered Abu no advice, nor did he try to dissuade him. In fact, he looked pleased to be rid of him.

Abu went on his way and very soon he was alone in the enormous plain. From time to time he lifted his face and gazed at the shimmering black spot ahead of him: Kurmin Rukiki. With every step he took, the forest seemed to retreat further into the grassland.

He had paused to rest, with his hopes mounting ever higher. He was glad he had so carefully kept the gourd that Tausayi's father had given him. Now that the wonderful sap was almost within reach, he had the right receptacle in which to place it, when he got it. The old man had told him that the substance was never to be touched by hand.

CHAPTER TEN

THE FOREST OF DEATH

For two months Abu walked on. All the time the black mass in the distance seemed to mock his efforts. Try as he would, it never seemed to get any nearer. He fed on forest fruits until his tongue was sore. He tramped until his feet blistered and healed again.

At last he saw a pillar of smoke rising out of the Kurmi. His hopes mounted. A new energy flooded his entire body, and he did not pause for a moment until he came to the house from which the smoke arose. A man was skinning antelope near a fire. He was a great hulk of a man and his body was completely covered with hair. Abu was afraid to talk to him.

'Who are you?' the man roared out, reaching for his bow.

'I ... I am a poor traveller. I'm on my way to Kurmin Rukiki.'

The hairy man put down his bow and laughed for a long time. 'Ha, ha, ha! Yes, this is how they suffer! Here am I in this bush. For a year now I've not seen a human face; and then the first man I see wants to go and die in Kurmin Rukiki. Ha, ha, ha!'

A shiver ran down Abu's spine. 'Show me the ... the way,' he stammered.

'I'll show you soon enough. I'm a hunter in this district, but there's a certain limit beyond which I may not travel. I will take you there when I'm ready, but no further.'

The hunter housed Abu for seven days, nursing his sores, feeding him back to his proper weight, and all the time telling him to give up the idea of visiting Kurmin Rukiki.

Abu laughed as though the man were talking like a child. 'I did not go back when the Kurmin was yet a dream; now that I can almost touch it with my hands, you ask me to go back! Listen; on my way to this place I have been robbed, beaten, put in jail, my ear has been cut off, and yet ...'

'You're a brave man indeed.'

'Have no fear about my return. I have a strong reason for believing that I shall return.'

'And what is that?'

'My dear friend, it is a long story. I have been badly treated in this world just because I have no money.' He shook his head, and the hunter appeared so deeply sympathetic that he told him the story of Mallam Shehu.

'Do not try to dissuade me as you have done so far; it will be no use. I leave for Kurmin Rukiki tomorrow.'

The next morning the hunter led him to his limit and, with tears on his grisly, hairy face, shook his hand.

'I cannot go any further. Good luck; and may Allah bless you!'

Abu walked until well into the afternoon and at last arrived at the forest. It was a terrible forest, this Kurmin Rukiki. Even at midday no light penetrated into its depths, and it was completely trackless. Abu worked his way inside, through the thorns and stinging insects and snakes. He wandered about in it all day and at night he slept. For days on end he made little headway and at last it became clear to him that he would never know the right tree in such gloom, and among so many.

Abu wept. He had come thus far, he had borne untold suffering and was at last at the end of his journey; but where was the substance he sought? What was the use of carrying about the gourd if he was going to put nothing into it?

One night he was awakened by a brilliant glow; something was shining at the foot of a tree. Cautiously he made his way to the bright spot, and, with a sudden leap, lunged at it. But his hands came in contact with something cold and slippery – a python! With a yell he thrust it away and it thudded heavily to the ground.

Abu could not sleep that night. He walked about the forest unable to get the horror of the python out of his mind; every moment he expected it to attack him.

It was some days later when he again saw that glittering object. This time it was higher up in a tree, and Abu threw a stick at it. There was a mighty explosion. He was flung as high as the treetop, to land again on a carpet of spikes and insects. He lay there senseless for a long time. His mouth was battered and swollen, his face cut in many places. One of his eyes had been blinded, but he had not lost his precious gourd.

When he came out of his coma he was quite certain that he was going to die in the forest. He crawled to his knees, but fell back helpless. Two weeks passed, and nature seemed to have helped him recover his strength. He could stagger around on his feet, though his body was as stiff as wood.

Soon afterwards he stumbled blindly against the glittering object again. He pushed away from it, and, when he touched it, a gasp of surprise escaped him. In his hands was an old woman. She was so old that her body was shrivelled and her face one mass of wrinkles. The hair on her head was white as a bleached cloth, and she was weak with the burden of her years.

'My son,' she quavered, 'what is it that you are prepared to sacrifice so much for? What do you want in this enchanted forest of death?'

Abu mumbled his story all over again and the old woman told him how very sorry she was to hear it. 'I am going to give you this sap, not because you have been deprived of your rightful wife and want vengeance, but out of pity for your sufferings.' She went to a tree and made three marks on it. 'Have you got a container for the sap?'

Abu produced the gourd he had kept for so long, and she filled it for him.

'Run! Run out of this forest before I harm you! Quick!' As the

old woman spoke her face changed. Hair grew out around her eyes and her body took on the form of a leopard. She uttered a wild growl and chased the terrified Abu out of Kurmin Rukiki. He found his way back to the hunter's lair.

CHAPTER ELEVEN

A CHANGED MAN

The hairy hunter was very surprised to see him back. 'You're the first man ever to go into that wood and come back alive,' he declared.

Abu wasted no time there. As soon as it was dawn he made his way back to the home of Tausayi's father. He travelled for several months before he reached it, and, when he at last knocked at the old man's door and it was opened to him, all the people stared at him as if he were some monstrous stranger.

'Who are you?' came the old man's voice from within.

'I am the man whom your son sent to get some gum from a deadly tree in Kurmin Rukiki.'

'How can that be? The man who came here was young and handsome; he had two ears and two eyes.'

Abu felt ashamed of himself. 'Can you remember how long ago that was? Do you think you yourself are still as young as you were then? Sit down, man, and don't waste any more of my time. I am the man to whom you gave five pounds and a horse. Also a gourd. Now, all those things except only the gourd, were taken from me. This is not the time to ask me what happened. What you should ask is, "Did you get what you went for?" '

The old man was surprised, but still unconvinced. Then Abu put his hand into his clothes, and from his undergarments produced the charm that Tausayi had given him. 'Do you remember this?'

'Ah!' exclaimed the old man.

At once he ordered the servants to attend Abu and feed him as best they could. Abu remained there for four days, and then he said to Tausayi's father: 'I am ready to go. But first I have a duty to your son. Where is that brother of his whom he wanted to see?'

The man was called forth and that night due preparations were

made for the departure next day. Abu and Tausayi's brother left in the early hours of the morning, each man riding a horse, with a plentiful supply of money and provisions.

Tausayinka da Sauki did not recognize either his own brother or Abu Bakir. 'Who are you?' he asked.

'I am Abu Bakir whom you sent to Kurmin Rukiki. This is your brother. You remember my promise?'

At that Tausayi's hard face softened with joy. He asked: 'Is this how you have suffered?'

'What does that matter when I've got what I wanted?'

'You have got it?'

Abu produced the gourd and Tausayi looked at it with great happiness. Tausayi asked his brother about the family, and learnt that his mother was long since dead but that his father was still living. He gave the two travellers beds to rest upon. In the morning he prepared a parcel of clothes and food for his old father and bade farewell to his brother.

'I have not the courage to come back home,' he said. 'Give the old man my blessings. I have indeed wronged the community and cannot show my face before them. This town is the place for people of my kind who have fled from the evil they have done.'

The brother thanked him, and he went on: 'Whenever you can find the time, come and see me. Some day, perhaps, I may be able to come home.'

His brother left, and he set to work preparing Abu's medicine. He mixed the sap from the poisonous tree with a little antimony that women use for their eyes and a few other ingredients known only to him. He was careful not to touch the pure sap with his bare hands, but when the mixture was made, he said it was safe if quickly washed off.

'This is how you should use the mixture,' he said when he had finished. 'Do your best to rub it on the skin of Mallam Shehu's son. You can easily do that when the boy is asleep. At the same time, cut some hair from his head and bury it in a newly dug grave. That is all you need to do.'

'But how am I to do all this without being seen?'

'I have thought of that. I have here,' said Tausayi, holding up a black talisman, 'what we call *layan zana*. With this on your person, you can go where you will and no one will see you. You will be invisible.'

'Is that all I have to do?'

'Yes.'

'And what is your fee?'

'My only fee is the punishment which will be upon your own head; just as we agreed from the first. Goodbye.'

Abu went back to his native Galma.

His mother did not know him any longer. She had grown old, and he himself had become so disfigured that no one recognized him. His elder brother, whom he had told to take care of her, stared at him as though he were a stranger. Abu spoke to him, and, as soon as she heard his voice, his mother ran up to him and embraced him.

'Abu Bakir! Can this be you? With one eye, and one ear? Oh, my son!'

Weeping, she led him into the house and put a pot on the fire. She boiled water for a bath and when he had cleaned himself there was great rejoicing within the family. He and his brother were soon left alone to exchange old memories.

'Your friend Zainobe has got a child. He's such a lovely boy that you cannot fail to like him. He passes here every morning on his way to school. As soon as you see him, you will recognise him.'

'Is that so?' rejoined Abu, pretending not to be much interested. He told none of his family how he had fared on his journey, but remarked carelessly: 'Will you show the boy to me when he passes here?'

Next morning when Zainobe's son was passing on his way to school with ten other boys. Abu's brother called him out to see him. Abu ran out and was amazed to see how big and handsome the boy had grown. The boy greeted them, and passed on his way. Abu went back into the house and cautioned his mother and brother not to reveal his identity to anybody in the town.

'If anybody in this town knows that I'm back, it will be terrible for you. I shall kill both of you, and still do what I intend to do.'

Mother and son were startled, but said nothing.

'Where does this boy sleep?' Abu asked.

Abu's brother said, 'His father has built him a house in the middle of the courtyard, and no one else goes into it. There he sleeps. But why do you ask?'

'Oh, it's nothing.'

CHAPTER TWELVE

THE MADNESS OF KYAUTA

At night Abu Bakir put on his layan zana talisman that was said to render a man invisible. He went into the room where the boy slept. He smeared him with the magic preparation, and with a pair of scissors cut off some hair from his head. He mixed this hair with the preparation, washed his hands, and then went to the house where Zainobe slept. Placing a hand on her, he shook her.

'Zainobe!'

Zainobe turned in her sleep.

'Get up. It is I, your true husband, Abu Bakir.'

She stared through sleep-dimmed eyes like one hypnotized. Because of the layan zana, she saw nothing. His voice came in a drone.

'Listen to what I have to say. You have disgraced me. You have caused me untold suffering. It is written that you shall pay for all this in this world. Your present husband took you away from me because he wanted a son. That son shall be a curse to you.'

He left her abruptly, and with his back against the wall seemed to melt into the night.

As soon as he was outside, he made his way to the graveyard where he buried the hair of Kyauta, Zainobe's son. Zainobe awoke soon after, trembling with fear.

'I've had a terrible dream!' she screamed, going at once to make sure that her son was still alive. She found Kyauta fast asleep, breathing peacefully. Zainobe sighed with relief, and went back to her bed. But morning found her still sleepless. It would have been silly to recount what she imagined was a dream so she told no one about it.

That morning Kyauta did not come as usual to greet his parents. He got up, and, without washing his feet in the water which his mother kept for him in the kettle, went into his father's house and took two shillings from the sheepskin. With this he went towards the main gate, and when the guards questioned him he said: 'Where am I going? What business is it of yours? Am I a thief?'

'But you have never got up so early; you've never spoken so rudely to us.'

'Nonsense! Let me pass.'

The startled gatemen shrank back and Kyauta swept past them. He made his way straight to the bicycle shed in the middle of the town, and having paid two shillings took a cycle out and began to ride it aimlessly through the streets.

Zainobe thought the boy had gone to see his father, while Mallam Shehu thought that Kyauta was detained by his mother. When Mallam Shehu got up, he went to the bathroom, saw the unused water which Zainobe had placed for the boy, but not a sign of his son. At last he went into his wife's room.

'Zainobe, what are you doing there with Kyauta? Don't you know it is time for school? Why do you keep him?'

The woman came out at once and replied: I thought the boy was with you. Did you not send for him?'

The old man whistled. He went indoors, sweeping his large gown before him. Next he went to the gate and asked the men on guard whether they had seen Kyauta.

'Yes, we have seen him. It was very early in the morning, and he spoke very rudely to us. We thought he was going to school, but it was too early. We were surprised at his behaviour.'

'And you didn't stop him?'

'Why should we? We thought you might have sent him.'

Mallam Shehu at once sent a man to the school, but there the teacher told them that the boy was not present; in fact, the teacher himself was on the point of sending someone to find out whether there was something the matter with the boy.

Shehu sent people all over the town, and at last the boy was found in the company of the bicycle hirers, people known for their loose manners and feckless outlook upon life. He was dragged home. and his father asked him: 'Why did you deceive the gateman? Why did you not tell them you were running away from home?'

He said nothing.

'Do you know who took two shillings I placed on my sheepskin?'

'I object to being questioned in this manner! Do you keep me

in the house as a watch-man? I don't know anything about your wretched two shillings.'

Mallam Shehu was surprised at this rude reply, and Zainobe told him not to lose his temper but to give her a chance to speak privately to the boy. She thought she knew how to set about it.

She prepared him his favourite meal, stew with chicken, and laid out a clean table. Kyauta was in his room when her message reached him. 'Tell her I will be there soon.'

She waited and waited, but he did not come. So she sent the messenger again, and when Kyauta appeared he looked angrily at everything she had prepared for him. With his left hand he felt the food; then he faced her, his eyes blazing.

'This cold food for me! Am I a dog?'

He gave one kick to the table and all the crockery tumbled to the floor and was smashed to fragments. Zainobe began to cry. The dream of the previous night came back to her; perhaps Kyauta's changed attitude was part of what had been revealed to her. She watched her son's movements with some anxiety, but even then she did not notice when he slipped outside the compound.

It was later that afternoon when an infuriated mob gathered outside Mallam Shehu's gate, holding a bleeding Kyauta before them.

'He stole my donkey,' shouted a roughly dressed farmer. 'He gambled with it and lost it. Now the man to whom he lost it has sold it back to me. I want my money back.'

Without question Mallam Shehu paid the man his due, and the mob departed in peace. He took the boy indoors and placed him under lock and key. One thing worried him. He was a man who hated publicity, particularly the type of publicity which this boy was bringing him. He paid a number of strong men to take his son to school, and to bring him back when school was over. But even at school it was difficult to control him. He stole slates from one boy and sold to another; he cursed his friends' fathers and within a short time the attendance at the school had been reduced to less than half. The parents were withdrawing their children because of Kyauta.

Mallam Shehu spent sleepless nights trying to discover a way by which he could keep the boy under check. But every day the boy grew worse. All the medicine-men he called charged him

64

fabulous amounts, and after they had prescribed a course of treatment for him the boy grew rapidly worse. Very soon the villagers became tired of carrying reports of his misbehaviour to the father himself; they preferred to approach the king.

Because of all this Shehu dared not appear in public. He hid himself in his shame, and even within his own household the two other women spent most of their time laughing at him. They would giggle at Zainobe and say: 'Thank Allah we have no children! Rather than have thieves as children, we prefer to have none.'

One evening Kyauta stole a bag of money belonging to his father, and with a ladder scaled the wall around his father's house. He went to a drinking house, and the flatterers praised him as he distributed the money to them in handfuls. The women clung to him and played gentle music in his ears. He was distributing the last few shillings of more than a hundred pounds when three men entered the drinking house and seized him. They dragged him back to his father.

In the morning Mallam Shehu sent him under custody to his teacher. 'I leave him in your care,' was his message. 'Since he has determined not to respect me, I cannot keep him here. Let it not be said that I killed my own son.'

The teacher placed Kyauta under strict guard, and when the boy was not studying he was detained in a guarded room.

Soon reports came to Mallam Shehu that he son was rapidly improving in his behaviour, but the old man was sceptical. 'Let him remain there until he's quite cured of his madness.' But Zainobe pressed him to release the boy and, aided by the teacher, they soon won Shehu over.

Kyauta was allowed to follow the boys who went in the evening to collect fodder. The boys were cutting the long grass when the madness again came over Kyauta. He turned to them and said: 'Goodbye. I leave you in peace!' He put down the curved knife he had been using and bolted.

Mallam Shehu's biggest heartache at this time was the fear that Kyauta might land him in some public disgrace that would involve his appearing before kings. More than once the prophecy of Mallam Sambo came back to him. Would his son really prove a source of ill-luck and ruin for him?

Seven days after he had left the protection of his teacher, Kyauta appeared before his father's salesman in the market. He greeted the trader and said: 'My father sent me to you. We are holding a little festival in the house and ...'

'Come in and sit down! This is a great honour. Mallam Shehu's son visiting my market stall!'

Kyauta went into the stall and made himself comfortable. He said nothing about his intentions but sat quietly in a corner, watching the customers come and go. Presently the tradesman excused himself and went out. He had seen a man carrying a rare cloth which he had been wanting to buy for a long time.

When he came back to the stall, Kyauta was gone. 'Well,' he reasoned, 'I did not send for him. He came of his own free will. Why should I bother myself about his departure?' He raised the matting so as to obtain money with which to pay his dealer. Every penny which he had kept there was gone.

His suspicions at once went to the customers in the neighbouring stalls. He made the market-police arrest them, and they were taken before the magistrate. The suspected men said that they had seen a boy leave the stall rather hastily. They described him minutely, and every word they said to the tradesman gave an accurate picture of Kyauta.

'Do you know this boy?' asked the magistrate.

'Yes. He is the son of my master, Mallam Shehu.'

'How long have you known him? Can you vouch for his honesty?'

'I have known him since the day he was born. And as for his honesty ... well, is he not the son of the wealthiest man in the area?'

'So you think that because he's the son of the wealthiest man he cannot steal? I am sending people at once to arrest him.'

Policemen dispersed in various directions, and presently those of them who had gone to the gambling house returned with Kyauta in their midst. They found upon his person the sum of ten pounds.

'Did you remove this money from the market stall?'

'No, I didn't.'

'But you visited the trader today?'

'I did.'

'Where were you when he went away?'

'You ask me annoying questions. Are you trying to say that I stole something from him? Is he not my father's servant?'

'Why did you not tell him when you were ready to leave?'

66

'I was not feeling very well. I couldn't wait.'

'And you didn't leave a message?'

'Why should I? I came straight to this house where my friends offered to take care of me ...'

'By relieving you of the money.'

Kyauta was silent. The policemen were completely baffled.

'Listen, little boy. You are still very young; no one can send you to prison. Tell us the truth. No ill can come of it. The loss of the money is no fault of yours. You know that these traders are careless men ...'

Kyauta relented. 'All right! I took the money.'

The policemen asked the trader how much money he had kept under the mat, and he said fifty pounds.

'Was that the amount you took?' they asked Kyauta.

'Yes.'

'And where is the rest?'

'I have gambled it away.'

They took him and put him in the guardroom.

Mallam Shehu wept when he heard the news. 'I have always known that that boy would land me in trouble.'

He went at once to the market and paid his tradesman fifty pounds. His son was released and he took him home, placing him once again under lock and key. For three days he gave him no food to eat, but on the fourth he took him a little quantity of milk in a bowl. Zainobe's motherly heart was touched.

'Release him,' she begged. 'I promise to take care of him.'

Mallam Shehu refused but his wife persisted, telling him how Kyauta had improved, and how courteous he was. She kept on weeping and pressing him day after day, until at last his heart ºsoftened and he released the boy.

CHAPTER THIRTEEN

A LIFE OF CRIME

Four days later that strange kink in Kyauta's mind awoke again. Everybody was asleep, when a figure sneaked into Mallam Shehu's strong-room. Darkness seemed to suit the activities of this intruder for he stole quietly forward, feeling his way until his fingers encountered what he sought. Then glancing about to see that no one had awakened, he slipped down the steps. In three strides he gained the spot where a ladder awaited him. It was a simple matter to scale the wall and land noiselessly on the other side. The intruder put his head down and disappeared into the town.

At dawn Mallam Shehu went to his strong-room. The door was open, but everything seemed to be in order until ... he stopped and counted the money bags again. One was missing. He made his way at once to Kyauta's room. The boy was not there.

'Zainobe,' he bawled, 'Zainobe!' and when she came: 'This is how you look after our son, is it? You lie there sleeping and off he goes with a hundred pounds of mine.'

The woman tried to excuse herself, but Mallam Shehu's anger would not abate and presently he and Zainobe were quarrelling. They told each other the things that hurt most, while the other women giggled at them.

Zainobe told Mallam Shehu again and again: 'Remember, I did not want to marry you. You forced me!'

They did not speak to each other for many days. Neither of them had the courage to leave the courtyard and, when there was any great activity in the town, they dared not show their faces. Their friends rapidly grew fewer and fewer, and when at times business forced Shehu to appear in public he could not help noticing how the people jeered at him and pointed him out as the rich father of a thief.

Kyauta went to Kano and there he joined forces with a gang of smash-and-grab robbers who raided the white men's shops. He was, however, an amateur at this game, and within a week he was caught and sentenced to eight months' imprisonment.

About this time a man came to Galma to collect merchandise for sale at Kano, and he put up at the house of Mallam Shehu. His first question, when he had settled down was: 'How about that son of yours, Kyauta?'

'My son,' sighed Mallam Shehu, 'has caused me great suffering. He has become very bad. I'm ashamed to tell you of his activities. You won't believe it, but the son of Shehu, the richest man in Galma, has become a ... a thief!'

'But where is he now?'

Mallam Shehu shrugged his shoulders. 'Where is he? He went away with a hundred pounds of mine about a month ago. That's all I know.'

The trader chewed his kolanut for a long time before replying. 'I don't know this son of yours very well; I was present at the name-giving ceremony, and after that I saw him at his school. I am afraid to raise your hopes, but ... but I saw someone like him at Kano. Please, great Mallam, do not take offence, but he was ... he was among prisoners.'

'That must be him, then!' shouted Mallam Shehu. 'Offence? Have I not seen worse? He must be the one!'

For this news of his son, Shehu received his guest with wide-open arms. When the merchant was going back to Kano, he gave him a servant to accompany him and trace his son.

Arriving at Kano, the merchant led the servant to an incinerator where the prisoners were to work. They waited for a long time before the prisoners came, and the trader at once spotted Kyauta among them. He had picked up a cigarette stub and was smoking it, when the warder beat him on the back.

'Kyauta!' he whispered, 'Kyauta! I wish to speak to you.'

Kyauta turned. His eyes were yellow and his face very thin. 'You can't. Go and see the warder, and give him a little tip.'

The merchant went to the warder that night, and having bribed him told him his intentions. The warder said, 'Come and wait for us by the bush where we always work. You will then be able to speak to Kyauta.'

Promptly at the time arranged the prisoners turned up. Kyauta and the merchant were given the opportunity to be alone for some time.

The merchant said: 'Your father has sent me to you.'

'Is he well?'

'Yes, and so is your mother.'

'What is your message? Has he sent me any money?'

'No, he hasn't. He wants to know how long you have to serve, so that this servant may lead you back to him.'

'I have three months more,' Kyauta lied, knowing well that he had only one more month.

The merchant went about his work and sent the servant back to Galma with the news. In a month Shehu's servant returned to wait two months for the release of the boy. That night he took gifts to the warder and expressed his intention of speaking to Kyauta on the morrow.

'You're very lucky,' said the warder, pocketing the money. 'You won't have to speak to your master's son in secret.'

'What do you mean?'

'He was released today. He told me he was going to visit friends. I can tell you where to find him.'

The servant took the address, but wandered vainly about the town for six nights and seven days without finding him. He was running short of money when he finally gave up. He returned to Galma and related the story in detail to Mallam Shehu.

For his part, Kyauta had gone to another town where he had met a clerk working for an English firm. The clerk had taken an instant liking to him and engaged him as a servant and shop assistant. Kyauta in his new role was very helpful and capable; even the clerk's wife could not speak highly enough of his honesty and humility. The clerk himself grew to trust him so much that he would leave him in charge of the shop and when he returned everything would be in order. One day Kyauta made a proposition to the clerk.

'You have been working for these English people for a long time. Have you ever thought of planning a business of your own?'

'Yes,' the clerk admitted, wondering what the boy would say next.

'My sole desire is to help you. It is this: I want you to buy things cheaply from the shop and give them to me to sell for you. I am a native of these parts; I'll find it very easy to make good profits, with my knowledge of the people and their ways.'

The clerk at once agreed. He packed up goods to the value of fifteen pounds and gave them to Kyauta to sell. Kyauta went into the interior and made a profit of well over five pounds on the sale. He returned the money to the clerk and his wife pointed this out as further proof of the boy's honesty. That night she spoke to her husband.

'Since we came up here to live, we've never met such an honest boy as Kyauta; let us do something to help him.'

'It is a good idea,' said the husband.

They prepared another bundle for him and gave it to him to sell. This time the value was twenty pounds, and the boy far exceeded the profits expected of him.

'Instead of travelling up and down the country in this manner,' Kyauta proposed, 'why not open a shop in that area? As far as I can see, the people are quite willing to buy things, but there's no one to supply them.'

The clerk hesitated, but his wife drove away his fears.

They gave him the money next day; enough to build a good shop. In two months he was back, and the clerk's wife then accompanied him to the interior to see what sort of a job he had made of it. She was very satisfied with the work.

They returned, and shifted articles to the new branch. And that was the time when Kyauta looked up to the sky and thanked his Allah. 'At last! I have found what I want.'

He opened the shop, and, left completely alone, he spent whatever money he made on gambling. Flatterers never left his house, and his stables were never short of horses.

At the end of the month the clerk asked him to render an account, but he said that things were in such a mess that monthly accounts would not be possible for some time. At the end of the next month he still had no account ready. The clerk's wife began to get suspicious. She urged her husband to send someone at once to the branch shop.

'Let him collect whatever money the boy can give him; if you let him go on in this manner, you will get into trouble with the firm.'

The messenger got there and found the shop completely empty; the boy had not a penny upon his person and even the

flatterers had deserted him. He went back and told the clerk what he had seen.

Kyauta was sitting in the empty shop one cool morning when three policemen appeared before him.

'We have come to arrest you,' they told him quietly.

He followed them without the least resistance. One of the policemen remained behind to lock the shop doors and Kyauta turned round and said to him: 'There's no need. The goods there are not worth more than ten shillings.'

They took him to the court and tried him. The magistrate recognized him at once as the boy whom he had sentenced to eight months' imprisonment at Kano some time previously.

Nothing could be done with him until his father appeared on his behalf and paid the clerk the sum of four hundred pounds, the estimated value of the shop's contents, and a substantial fine to the court. The clerk was glad to escape conviction, and balancing his books, swore never to trust any stranger for the rest of his life. Kyauta accompanied his father back to Galma.

As soon as the gate closed behind them, Mallam Shehu put the boy in chains and handcuffed him.

CHAPTER FOURTEEN

THE HAND THAT FED HIM

His stay at Kano had converted Kyauta into a robber of the first calibre. He had learnt how to slip handcuffs from his wrist. For the first day he grudgingly tolerated this parental captivity. On the second day he was restless. Before evening handcuffs and chain were lying on the floor and he himself was sitting in a train bound for Lagos.

In Lagos he met a man called Dogo. Dogo was a giant of a man, tall and muscular, and a dreaded figure in the society of robbers. He and Kyauta were well-suited to each other and within a moment of their meeting they had decided to join forces. Kyauta admired Dogo for his complete fearlessness. Many were the tales of gaol breaks which Dogo told his new confidant. The gaol-house had the advantage for Dogo that it provided him with clean clothes, tolerable food and shelter, just when he needed these things most.

'Only a fool fears the law,' said Dogo. 'If they catch you, go with them! You know when you're fed up with them. That is the time to make your get-away.'

When Mallam Shehu found the discarded handcuffs and chain, he almost wept with frustration. His shoulders bowed in deep thought, he made his way slowly to Zainobe's room. There was no plan which had not entered his mind for the destruction of this worm that was eating away his son's better self. He had paid large sums of money to seers; he had hired special guards to watch him minutely; he had offered him the best protection that a father had ever offered to a son who had been born after thirty-five years of married life.

'Zainobe, I am tired. I am sick of hiding myself in my own town. Better to go elsewhere – to a place where I'm not known – and make a fresh start, than to continue under this burden of shame.'

The woman refused to leave Galma. For two whole days he tried to bring her round to his own point of view.

'If you do not go with me, what else can you do? You can't go back to your parents. Your father will not have you. You can't remain in my own household. The other women would kill you in a week. What else can you do but follow me? If you don't ...'

'I will go with you,' Zainobe whispered.

Mallam Shehu sold all his things, and changed his money into notes.

He took with him a little box and two horses, one for himself and one for Zainobe. Before he finally departed he went to the king and told him he was going on a pilgrimage to Mecca. His other wives he left in the care of his chief servant, and set off into the desert.

Zainobe and Mallam Shehu travelled until they had crossed seven deserts and seven oases and then they came to a town. Nobody from Galma could ever boast that he had travelled that far before. Shehu reported himself to the king of the town, saying that he proposed to remain there as a trader.

'What is your name?' asked the king.

'Mallam Usuman.'

'From where?'

'Daraman.'

The king liked him for his humility and good looks. He leased out an area to him, and bade him good luck. While still under the

king's protection, Mallam Shehu built on the area, and soon afterwards moved there himself. That gift of making money, which Kyauta had all but killed, awakened again and within a few years of his arrival he had begun to pile up money in heaps. His name travelled far and wide as a man of wealth and good breeding.

Kyauta used to travel between Lagos and Accra on his raids. He was caught and imprisoned many times, but Dogo's philosophy had sunk so deeply into him that every time he went into jail he came out with stronger determination to do worse things. At last the Lagos police grew tired of seeing his face, and he and Dogo were repatriated to some town which they said was their home.

They continued their wanderings, until one day they reached the town where Kyauta's father lived. They put up a shelter in the hills and from there organized raids on the town.

One afternoon they dressed in their best like respectable mallams and took a walk round the town. They passed by a compound which struck them with its magnificence and the general impression of immense wealth which it suggested.

'Who is it that lives there?' Kyauta asked a passer-by.

'A man called Usuman. He came here six years ago with a woman and a few things. Now look what Allah has done for him!'

Kyauta and Dogo winked at each other. On their way back to the hills they bought a coil of strong rope, and that night they put on their 'working clothes': a pair of trousers with room in the belt for a knife.

They found it easy enough to scale the wall. They knew from long experience exactly where the strong-room was likely to be. Kyauta was in the lead; he was crossing the threshold when he heard a strange noise. Looking into the darkness ahead of him, he noticed that the man lying on the bed had sprung up and was slipping into the shadows – away from the moonbeams which poured into the room.

He kept his eyes fixed on the man in the shadows; he could see, too, that the man was crouching as if ready to fight. There he crouched, his eyes glowing defiantly. But strangely enough, Kyauta could make no move. As he said later, 'Something seemed to have held my legs and hands; I couldn't move. I could hardly breathe.'

As he stood there dumbfounded, Dogo brushed him aside and

with a yell sprang upon the house-owner. Kyauta watched them struggling. Dogo called out, 'Hurry, Kyauta! I am holding his throat. Bring your knife!'

Kyauta gave a start. More to please Dogo than to obey his own will, he drew his knife and stabbed. At that moment a door opened and a fair face peered at them.

'Run!' shouted Dogo. Dropping knife and man, they ran for it. Kyauta dashed blindly into the arms of the intruder who clung to him with all her might. They were standing in the moonlight and, as he thrust her back, a gasp of astonishment escaped him.

'My mother!' he exclaimed.

'My son!' shouted Zainobe.

They embraced, Kyauta holding her with his bloodstained hands. 'What brought you here?' he asked. 'Is my father dead?'

'I came here with him. But, my son, why steal in your father's house?'

'My father's house? I thought you were at Galma.'

'We left there many years ago. We could not stand the ravages you had done to our good name.' Her eyes filled with tears and she buried her head on his breast.

Dogo said: 'Leave that woman alone, and let us take what we want to take. You have always let women land you in jail. Leave her alone.'

Kyauta smarted under Dogo's words. How could he tell a worthless robber, friend though he was, that he had robbed his own mother? 'Have patience, Dogo,' he said lightly. 'I'll soon be finished with her.'

'Have you done anything, so far?' Zainobe asked.

'We have broken into the strong-room. A man was trying to oppose us, and of course ... well ... what do you think? Dogo held him, while I cut his throat. He lies dead now. No more trouble from him.'

'You killed him?' Zainobe whispered.

She ran towards the room with Kyauta following at her heels. They struck a light, and found a body lying there. It was Mallam Shehu, Kyauta's own father. He was quite dead.

'You have killed your own father. You know the fate of a murderer, Kyauta. If you have anywhere to run to, better run now.'

'I'll run. But first let me remove the rope by which we entered this compound.' They removed the rope from the wall, then

Zainobe opened a secret door and let him out into the night. Then she shouted: 'Thief! Thief!'

Dogo made at once for the spot where the rope hung, and there he found the wall blank. He wheeled round to face a compound teeming with the king's best policemen. Hearing the king's friend was in trouble they had poured into the compound in their dozens. They caught Dogo at once, and he kept shouting: 'We were two! We were two! ...'

Policemen dispersed all over the compound, bent on discovering who the accomplice could be. They went into room after room until they came to that in which Mallam Shehu lay.

'You're sure you were two?' they asked Dogo. 'I swear by Allah.'

'What is the name of the second robber?

'Kyauta.'

'You are telling a lie.'

They bound him up and removed him. Zainobe was weeping.

CHAPTER FIFTEEN

THE LAW IS FULFILLED

Kyauta fled to his hillside shelter. Now that his father was dead – killed by his own hands – a sudden change came over him. The spell was broken. Kyauta, who normally knew no fear, was now afraid to run away, lest they seized his mother and executed her.

He heard that Dogo had confessed to the murder of Mallam Shehu and that Dogo had been kept in the prison yard to await execution.

One afternoon Dogo went to draw water from the well. He slipped and falling down a hundred and eighty feet crashed into the water below. Nobody knew whether it was an accident or his fear of the hangman's rope.

Zainobe too had been altered by her sorrows. She was thin and pale, a mere shadow of her youthful days. There were times when, seated alone, the memory of that 'dream' she had had some years back would come vividly before her. She would see Abu Bakir speaking to her, telling her that her son would bring her nothing but misery. And before she had quite gathered the threads of the dream, it would slip out of her mind.

As was the custom, she mourned for Mallam Shehu seven weeks. After this period she bathed herself and sent word to the king that she had something to say to him. She was brought before him and she told him of her son, the rightful heir to Shehu's property.

'He is in a distant land and it may be many days before he gets here; but I have sent a message to him.'

She held secret meetings with Kyauta and together they agreed upon the day when he should make his appearance.

'When you do come before him,' she advised him, 'remember that you're the son of Mallam Usuman: that is the name by which they knew him here.'

On the appointed day, Kyauta turned up and all who saw him were filled with sorrow at the close resemblance he bore to his father. They felt sorry for his mother who had suffered so much.

Kyauta shared out most of his father's money into three portions, giving one third to the king; the second portion to the blind, the lame, and the lepers; the last third he assigned to the building of a large mosque. On the day of his departure he went to see the king.

'I am ready to leave,' he said. 'I thank you for all the good things you did for my father. My heart is sad but a man must return to his native land.'

On their way home Zainobe told him that she had at last discovered the reason for his going bad in the way he had. She recounted the 'dream,' and how for many years she had been arguing with herself whether it had, indeed, been a dream.

'But now I am quite clear in my mind. It was not a dream. Abu Bakir came to me in my dream and hypnotized me. He must have done something terrible to you also.'

'Do you think so, mother?'

'I do not think; I am sure.'

They went quietly to Galma. Apart from the two wives of his father, nobody knew that they had returned. Kyauta divided his father's remaining property there among the women and sent them all away. Then he sharpened his sword.

'It is my turn,' he smiled, when his mother challenged him. 'There are no short cuts. When I have done it, you shall not see me for one year; but I shall return to look after you.'

His mother, already weak and pain-wracked from her sufferings, began to weep afresh and he smiled and comforted her. But she was still weeping when he made his way to the house of Abu Bakir.

Abu Bakir was sitting by the fire, writing Arabic figures on a wooden slate. He looked up when the stranger entered unannounced. Abu was now an old man, much disfigured, and with his one eye not very strong, he did not recognize the stranger who addressed him in menacing tone.

'I am Kyauta, son of Zainobe, the woman who was to have been your wife.'

Abu Bakir looked up startled, and the slate dropped out of his hands.

'I have come to kill you,' Kyauta said.

Abu stared at him; then he tried to rise. With one sweep of the razor edged sword, the youth sent his head flying into the fire. Then Kyauta ran.

For one year he ran wild, eating wild fruits, hunting game, sleeping in the rain and in the sun. At the end of that time he came back to his mother.

He, too, had aged.

With the heart-broken woman, he lived in his father's former house, until the end of his days.

The moon was still shining when the old man completed his tale, but there was not even a glow in the fire. He gathered his robe about his knees and smiled.

'That is the end of my tale,' he mused. 'A most sorrowful tale, truly. Yes. A sorrowful tale. One must not take it upon oneself to inflict vengeance. But you can see the moral for yourselves.'

He glanced round at his listeners. They squatted like little cones of white, their heads between their knees. Quietly he rose and reached for the glistening coins on the sheepskin. Had he not warned them that they would all be asleep?

The coins chinked, and a voice said: 'Old man, don't do that. Have you won the bet?'

He started. One by one the cones took the shape of bright-eyed men who suddenly roared with laughter.

The old man had no alternative. He, too, laughed.